Fireman

Lost and Found

Photographs by John Walker

MAMMOTH

It was a lovely, sunny day. "I am going to have a party tonight," Bella said. "Why?" asked Sarah and James. "No reason," replied Bella, "just because I am happy."

"We'll help you," cried the twins excitedly. "First, I must go to the supermarket," said Bella. "Would you look after the café and my cat while I am gone?"

But Rosa the cat had a better idea and hid. Bella pulled her trolley to the bus stop. As Trevor helped her on to the bus, he said, "Your trolley feels a bit wobbly, Bella."

When Bella sat down she heard a noise. She looked inside
her trolley and there was her cat. "Oh, Rosa! Now you will
just have to come shopping with me." "Meow," replied Rosa.

At the supermarket, Bella said, "I must hurry as the shop will be closing soon." So Bella bought everything she needed and paid for it. "Good, now it's time to go home."

Just as they were leaving, Rosa jumped out of the trolley and dashed through the swing doors at the back of the supermarket. Rosa was hungry and could smell cat food.

"Oh, no!" cried Bella. "Naughty, naughty cat." She
followed Rosa through the swing doors and marched
down the stairs to the basement.

"Roșa, Roșa, good little kitty," called Bella crossly. "We must go home, the shop will be closing soon." Rosa was quite happy hiding behind some boxes of cat food.

Finally, Bella found her. "Oh, Rosa. I am glad to see you!" she cried. "You must never run away again! I am tired now and in a hurry so we shall have to take the lift."

The lift doors opened and Bella went in. The doors closed and she pushed the up button. Nothing happened. Bella pushed the button to open the doors. Nothing happened.

She was trapped in the lift. She picked up the emergency phone. To her surprise, a voice said, "Hello, may we help you?" "Oh, oh, I am trapped in a lift," shrieked Bella.

"Don't worry, Madam, we shall be right there," said the voice calmly. Bella sat down and put Rosa on her lap. Rosa stretched, purred, closed her eyes and went to sleep.

Down at the fire station, Station Officer Steele called
Fireman Sam and Elvis. "Come quickly, a woman is
trapped in a lift at the big supermarket in town."

The firemen jumped into Jupiter, the fire engine, and set off at once. "Who is it?" asked Sam. "I don't know, but she sounded upset."

The three firemen rushed into the empty supermarket.
"Look, there's the lift," said Fireman Sam. "The emergency
light is flashing. It must be stuck in the basement."

Fireman Sam managed to prise open the lift doors.
"If we put a piece of wood between the doors, it will
stop them from closing," explained Station Officer Steele.

"Now, let's see. How do we get down there?" muttered Station Officer Steele. "Why don't we use the ladder?" said Sam, pointing to it.

Sam and Steele peered down into the dark lift shaft.
"Hello! Hello!" they both called. "Is anyone there?
Hello!" Then they heard a voice shout out.

"Of course there is someone here! What a silly thing to ask! I am here!" Bella looked down at Rosa and said, "It's all right Rosa, we are going to be rescued."

Fireman Sam lowered his ladder on to the roof and bravely climbed down. Carefully he lifted the hatch on top of the lift. What a surprise he had!

"Why Bella!" exclaimed Fireman Sam. "And look who is with you!" "Yes, it's Rosa," smiled Bella. "But it is this naughty cat's fault that we were stuck in the lift."

Bella climbed carefully up the ladder, with Rosa under one arm. "Isn't this wonderful? We are free at last! Let's all go back to the café," she suggested.

"We could have been trapped all night," Bella smiled. "Now I know why I am having my party - to thank you for our rescue. We were lost and now we are found!"